# The 鶴 Crane Wife

Retold by Ena Keo

Illustrated by Cheryl Kirk Noll

STECK-VAUGHN®
COMPANY

*A Division of Harcourt Brace & Company*

www.steck-vaughn.com

# Contents

# Sachi Makes a Wish

As Sachi was walking home one night, a strong wind was blowing. Snow was coming down hard. He hurried to get home where it was warm. But there was not a wife waiting there for him.

Sachi felt so lonely. He made a wish for a wife. Suddenly, he heard a soft cry in the dark. He walked toward the sound. He found a beautiful white crane that had been hurt. "Don't be afraid. I'll help you," said Sachi.

Sachi carefully picked up the crane and carried it home. He gently cared for its broken wing. He kept it safe and warm until it grew strong and was able to fly again. Then one day, the beautiful white crane flew away.

Later, there was a knock at Sachi's door. He opened it to see a beautiful woman standing there. She bowed and smiled as if she knew Sachi. Then she asked him if she could be his wife. Sachi's wish for a wife had been granted!

Sachi was very thankful that the woman had come to him. He had waited a long time for a wife. Yukiko was her name. She was gentle and graceful. She was also very kind to Sachi.

After many months, Sachi could not find any work. He had no money. Sachi did not know what to do. Yukiko said she could help. She told him she could weave beautiful silk to sell.

Sachi was so happy that his wife could help. Yukiko said, "I will begin to weave the silk. But promise that you will not watch when I weave."

"Yes, dear wife, I promise," said Sachi.

Then Yukiko went away and began to weave. Later, she showed her silk to Sachi. It was beautiful and as light as feathers. He said it was the finest silk he had ever seen. Sachi took the silk to the market to sell.

The silk sold for a very high price. "I'm lucky to have such a clever wife," said Sachi.

He used the money to buy fine paintings and fancy new clothes. Sachi felt important in his new silk kimono. He liked having money. He asked Yukiko to weave more silk for him.

Yukiko wove more silk for Sachi. He kept his promise and did not watch her weave. Each time Yukiko wove silk, it was even more beautiful than the time before.

Sachi's silk was different from the rest. Everyone at the market wanted to buy it.

Sachi asked Yukiko to weave more and more silk. Sachi grew very rich. But Yukiko grew very pale and tired.

Before long, Sachi had spent all of his money. He went to Yukiko and asked her to weave silk again. Sachi said, "I promise, this is the last time I will ask. I will save this money."

Yukiko asked Sachi to repeat his promise to save the money. She also reminded him of his promise not to watch her weaving. Then Yukiko set to work. Click, clack, click, clack went the loom all night long.

Sachi grew tired of waiting for Yukiko to finish weaving. He waited as long as he could. Finally, Sachi could not wait any longer. He had to see how his wife was weaving the beautiful silk. He opened the doors to Yukiko's room. He saw a beautiful white crane weaving silk on a loom!

## Sachi Is Alone Again

Sachi couldn't believe his eyes. Yukiko was really the crane he had saved! The crane cried out, "You said that you would not watch me weave. Why did you break your promise?"

The crane sighed, "Now I must leave you." She lifted her wings and flew out the door. Sachi knew it was too late. He had driven her away.

Many lonely weeks passed for Sachi.
It would soon be spring in the village.
The cherry blossoms were in bloom.
Everyone was happy except for poor,
lonely Sachi. Every day, he searched
the sky for the beautiful white crane.
He never did find her.

**Moral:** Always keep your promises.